The Adventures of

Tilly

A Very Good Witch

Kat Walker

The Adventures of
Tilly
A Very Good Witch

Kat Walker

The Adventures of Tilly—A Very Good Witch
© 2024 Kat Walker

Publisher: Lilybet Press, Folsom CA
Editor: Linda Holderness

First printed: July 2024

ISBN: 9798333431042

"You got involved with a witch, and when you do that ... weird stuff happens."

— *Uncle Arthur, "Bewitched"*

"Come with me and you'll be
in a world of pure imagination."*

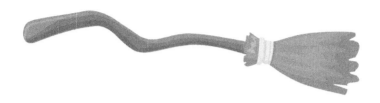

For My Grandsons

Made-up stories at bedtime have always been a family tradition. Starting with my son, we created adventures that guided him through his childhood. When he became a father, he introduced his twin sons to the magic of storytelling.

When the boys have sleepovers, I am always excited to share what I have written or we work together to create the next chapter of Tilly's adventures.

This book is dedicated to my grandsons A and B. Your imagination will carry you through your lives and continue to lead you to the next adventure.

Remember to always let your light shine.

---

*Lyrics from *Pure Imagination (Willy Wonka and the Chocolate Factory)* by Leslie Bricusse and Anthony Newley, 1971.

The Adventures of Tilly a Very Good Witch

Tilly's Childhood

Tilamia Carruthers was raised by her father, Benedict Carruthers, who was one of the most powerful witches in the Magic Realm. But Tilly and her father lived on Earth. As Tilly grew, she knew nothing about Supernatural beings. Her father kept that side of their lives a secret. She was raised as a normal human child and her father never used his magic in her presence.

Her father always seemed sad and very serious. All Tilly wanted with her whole heart was to see her father smile. She would recite funny stories to him, wear her clothes backward, anything she could think of to get him to smile.

She knew he loved her because each time she performed any of her silly antics, he would gather her in his arms and whisper, "Tilly, I love you so very much." But a smile never passed his lips.

She knew she should have a mother — everyone else did. She asked her father about her. There were no pictures of her, only portraits of her mother and father. When she asked him, he would answer that her mother had to go away almost the moment she was born, and they must hope she would return to them someday. He promised her that her mother never stopped loving her and was always holding her in her heart.

Benedict was the best father a little girl could ask for. They had a beautiful home, and Tilly never wanted for anything. Everything she wanted appeared if she just mentioned it to her father.

They both had good health and wealth. Her father was tall, strong, and very handsome. He didn't work at a job like her friends' parents did, and he was always there when she needed him. Tilly was just a happy, beautiful, healthy, normal eight-year-old girl.

One morning, Tilly woke to the smell of a yummy breakfast with all her favorites. She dressed quickly and practically flew down the stairs. Her father usually served a good and healthy breakfast with just poached eggs and oatmeal, so this was quite a treat. The table was filled with all her favorites: blueberry pancakes, sausage, strawberries, juice, scones, and berry muffins.

Her father just stood there with his very serious face. "Tilly, I have something very important to discuss with you after breakfast. But first, sit with me and let's enjoy our time together."

Tilly couldn't help but wonder and worry what his words meant. Breakfast was soon over, and Tilly's father was looking even more serious, if that could even be possible.

"My sweet little Tilly," he said. "I know you have always wondered about your mother, and I could never find the right words to explain to you where she is without revealing my promise to her before she was taken from us. So here is the story of what happened before and after you were born."

Benedict explained: "Your mother and I

are both powerful witches. We come from generations of witches. We are also known as Supernaturals. Most of our kind don't live here on Earth. We live in another dimension known as the Magic Realm.

"Your mother and I met when we were children and knew then we would always be together. Your mother is very lovely with honey golden hair and emerald eyes just like yours. Her name is Rosalynne. She is one of the kindest, sweetest, and most powerful witches I have ever known. I still love her as much as the day I met her when we were young.

"As we grew older it was clear to all who knew us that we were deeply in love, and we would eventually be married. Both of our parents were delighted with the prospect.

"But one day a terrible misunderstanding over magic gone wrong caused our parents to disagree. Lives had been lost because of that spell gone wrong. My father and mother were held responsible. Your mother and I were forbidden to see each other, and certainly there would be no marriage.

"My parents were banished to the Dark

Realm, and I was banished to Earth for the remainder of my days.

"Now, as I said, your mother was a powerful witch and found a way to slip through a portal. A portal is usually used by non-Supernaturals when they have been allowed to visit the Magic Realm. She thought by using the portal, she could not be detected when she came to.

"We found each other soon enough and then we got married. We were always very careful to not use our magic. If we did, we knew we risked being discovered and she would be forced to go back.

"Then we learned we were having a baby girl! You! Our beloved Tilly. You were the brightest light in our lives."

He paused here and wiped tears from his eyes. Tilly ran to him and climbed into his lap. She was crying too.

"Father, what happened then?" Tilly asked. "Where is my mother now?"

"Your mother and I vowed on the day you were born that we would conceal your magic for a while, just until you were old enough and strong enough to handle the power that it would bring to you." He held her tightly.

"But your little light of magic kept shining through, so your mother cast a spell that your gifts would not come again till you were an adult. You should expect to feel your power in your twentieth year."

Tilly thought: *I'm eight now. I won't be twenty for twelve more years.* *

Her father went on: "Even though we hid ourselves deep in the mountains, your little light of magic and the spell your mother cast were like beacons to her parents. They found us almost immediately. We hid you in a drawer so they wouldn't know about you. They were very angry at your mother for disrespecting their wishes. Your mother was banished to the Dark Realm. That is where she is to this day."

He paused for a moment.

"So now we come to the most important thing I must tell you. I have found where she is in the Dark Realm, and I intend to rescue her and my parents, your grandparents. I also have the proof needed to show that my father had nothing to do with the tragic spell and I intend to have him forgiven. There is a new king in the Magic Realm, and I am certain he will listen."

And then she saw the most incredible thing ever on her father's face, his smile!

"I have arranged for a nice couple to move in and care for you until I return," he said. "They even have two children, so you will have playmates. They are humans, so there will be no talk of magic. Do you understand?"

Tilly nodded her head and held him tighter.

"Everything is going to be all right," her father said. "I will be home before you know it. There is nothing to worry about."

Only there was plenty to worry about.

THE HUMAN family arrived in a big noisy minivan. Ezra Mcguire, the father, was a big man with red blotches on his cheeks. He was smiling but his greedy eyes were already glancing from here to there, taking in all the nice things in their new temporary home.

His wife Charlotte was tall and thin and wore her hair pulled back in a tight ponytail.

She quietly placed her finger on a table as if inspecting for any dust to be found.

Their oldest child was a boy named Chad. He appeared to be about six. His little snotty nose was runny from a cold, and he was squirming to be released from his mother's hand. Then there was Darla — she was just five. She hid behind her father, hugging his legs while making a mean face at Tilly.

Tilly glanced at her father, hoping he would change his mind. She didn't have a chance to persuade him to just let her take care of herself.

She didn't need these people in their home!

Even though she was eight, she could cook her own meals and get herself to school on time. What could go wrong?

But it was too late. After introductions were made and hands were shaken, her father handed over bank account information to Ezra and the keys to the house.

Her father then turned to her. "Tilly, I will be back as soon as I can. It shouldn't be more than a few weeks. Be a good girl and remember not to talk about you-know-what! I love you."

He hugged her tightly and then he was gone.

Charlotte dropped Chad's little hand and set him free. Immediately the boy bolted from the room and crashing noises could be heard from around the corner. This caused Ezra to become completely red faced as he began to yell for his son to "get back here!"

So began the downward life of Tilly.

LIVING WITH the Mcguire family started off well enough. In the beginning they seemed to respect her needs of food, clean clothes and getting to and from school on time.

Oh, how she missed her father's loving hugs, though. She would happily have traded his serious face for the secret sneers she often caught on the faces of Ezra and Charlotte when they thought she wasn't looking.

She was always polite and helpful, not a bit like the Maguires' own children, who were always breaking things around the house and shouting back at their parents, which always led to the parents shouting back at them and then at each other. Tilly yearned for the peaceful house she once lived in.

Time passed. After the first three weeks, Tilly watched the front door, waiting with anticipation of finally meeting her mother and knowing that at last her father would smile and be joyful again.
But the three weeks turned into three months, and then two years passed.
Tilly was now twelve years old. She felt abandoned. There had been not one single word from her father, and Tilly had no idea where or how to look for him.

One day she overheard Ezra and Charlotte speaking in low voices at the kitchen table. Charlotte asked: "It's been so long since he left, surely he would have contacted us by now. Maybe something happened? Not that I am complaining much — we have everything we ever dreamed of. All the money in the world, thanks to his bank account!"

"Yep," Ezra agreed. "It's just too bad we must put up with little Miss Perfect, though.

I think it's time we taught her what life is really like, don't you? I think she should start taking over all your kitchen chores to start with. She is old enough to cook and clean."

You could almost hear the wheels turning in Charlotte's head.

"Why yes! It would give me more time for shopping and for spa days," she said excitedly. "And we could take our children for outings more often."

"Tilly! Get your lazy butt in here!" Ezra shouted. Ezra seemed always to be shouting about something. Tilly took her time entering the kitchen. She wouldn't want them to know she was eavesdropping on them.

"Yes sir?" she asked.

"It's been two years since your father abandoned you. Two years that we have been stuck with taking care of you, his ungrateful brat. It's time for you to take up some responsibility."

He sneered. "From now on you will be in charge of the kitchen. That will include all the cooking and cleaning. You should be able to take that on while still going to school."

As time passed, Tilly began to take on more and more household chores. The house was quite large, with all its bedrooms and bathrooms. But she managed it and kept her grades up as well. Her greatest and only joy was visiting the flower garden. While she did find time to prune, plant and weed, it always felt like the grounds almost took care of themselves.

The family that was supposed to be taking care of her became more and more needy and greedy. The children were constantly breaking and damaging the house. Their parents were not concerned enough to repair the broken windowpanes, the holes in the walls, and water damage from the constant overflows in the tub.

All they seemed concerned with was what they could buy next with their seemingly endless flow of money from Benedict's bank account.

This was Tilly's life. Year after year, going to school and returning home to take care of her house the best she could, catering to the demands of the family who was supposed to be caring for her, and providing a loving safe home for her while father was away.

Soon Tilly turned 18 and completed high school. There were no plans made for her to go to college. She had brought up the subject with her foster parents only to be scoffed at. They made it clear that her father's money would not be wasted on an education for her. She should get a job just like everyone else. In fact, they felt it was time for her to live on her own.

Since she would no longer be living there with them, they would have to take over the care of the house all by themselves and would almost certainly need every penny of the unlimited cash flow her father had provided.

Still, Tilly believed that her father would rescue her mother and grandparents and her family would all be together. She had to trust her father's promise. So, she packed up what she could carry and left her home behind, trusting that her father would find her when they returned.

WHAT TILLY and the Mcguires didn't know was that when Tilly left her home, it broke the spell over the never-ending supply of money in the bank provided to the Mcguire family for her care.

The moment she left, the account ceased to exist. It was as if it never existed. Imagine greedy Ezra's reaction when he arrived at the bank to demand his weekly cash and the bank officers told him they had no idea what account he was referring to. They had never heard of a Mr. Carruthers and they certainly did not recognize Ezra, either.

Imagine his anger and frustration when the security guards escorted him out of the bank, empty-handed and speechless. Imagine how he tried to explain to his wife and children that there was no more money.

The Mcguire family tried to live in the house for a while longer, but it seemed as if they had suddenly been cursed. First, Charlotte tripped on the sidewalk and broke her arm.

Then, Ezra developed a bad cough that just wouldn't go away. The doctor warned him he was having a reaction to black mold and should check the house for water damage for the source.

Then the children were attacked by dozens of angry wasps while relaxing on the front porch. It turned out they were highly allergic to the stings and nearly died from the reaction.

With their golden ticket no longer available, the family finally packed up and left.

THE HOUSE was suddenly empty except for the pixies that no one knew about. No one could see or hear them because they were also Supernaturals and had always lived with Tilly and her father. They had been watching over Tilly and her garden the best they could. They had created all the hardships for that nasty family who had driven Tilly out of her own home. Here, they would patiently wait for her return.

Like most young people on their own for their first time, Tilly found it wasn't easy. Jobs were scarce and didn't pay much. But she survived for the next couple of years:

Sometimes it was easy and sometimes it was tough.

This was one of those times that were tough. She didn't have a real job and was homeless. In fact, it was probably the worst she had ever been. She lived in a large cardboard box behind a restaurant. She washed dishes for the restaurant for food and bathroom privileges.

As her twentieth birthday drew closer, she didn't know what to expect. She had no one to ask what might come. She only knew that her father had told her that when she turned 20 that her powers would begin.

What kind of powers?

Would she turn green like the witch in the Wizard of Oz?

Tilly wished she knew a Supernatural or two or even how to find one. She had so many questions.

On the day of her twentieth birthday, Tilly realized she didn't have to wonder any longer. Her birthday turned into one of the most amazing days of her whole life.

Tillys Twentieth Birthday

Tilly woke to the sound of a voice outside her box.

"Good morning, Tilly!" the voice said.

Another voice could be heard: "Oh dear. What if she can't understand us yet? The pixies said today is the day she will understand us, and we can wish her a happy birthday and show her the way! Oh, for goodness's sake Tilly, wake up! We have so much to show and tell you!"

Now both voices were talking at the same time.

Tilly opened her eyes. Nope, she wasn't dreaming. Same cardboard box, same stinky clothes, same going-to-bed-hungry feeling.

"All right, who is out there?" Tilly sighed.

She crawled out of her box to find two

squirrels sitting up on their hind legs.

"Good morning, Tilly, and a very happy birthday to you!" the squirrels said at the same time.

"Uh ... I must still be dreaming," Tilly said to herself. "Who ever heard of talking squirrels?"

She recognized the squirrels, nonetheless. She often fed them with bits of her own meals. They lived in the big tree at the end of the alley, along with 123 other squirrels who were the rest of their family.

"Well, you couldn't understand us until today," said one of the squirrels.

The other squirrel added, "But today and from now on you can understand all animals. It's your first birthday gift!"

"Happy, happy birthday!" Both squirrels began to jump up and down in excitement. "Now get your shoes on and follow us. There are some others that you must meet, and you have places to go and things to do."

Tilly pulled on her sneakers and stood up. "This is crazy, you know, but, OK ... I am in. Why not? It is after all my twentieth birthday."

The squirrels took off in a streak of fur and ran quickly down the alley and around the corner. Tilly followed as fast as she could — squirrels are pretty fast.

Finally, they stopped at a brick archway. The archway was very old and had always been in the neighborhood park. No one really knew how old it was, but it was so pretty no one had ever thought of removing it.

Tilly noticed two tiny people with wings, no taller than three inches each. One was a female, and she was lovely. Her long hair was blond and floated about her pretty face. Her dress looked like it was made from flower petals. The male was also about three inches tall and was very handsome. They both fluttered around her.

The little man landed gently on Tilly's shoulder and made room for his mate. "Good morning, Tilly, and happy birthday!" he said.

Then the little woman spoke: "My name is Peony, and this is my husband, Lance. You don't know us, but we know you very well. We have tended to you since you were a baby in your father's home."

"We are called pixies" explained Lance. Our main job is to tend to gardens and such. We were always there in your garden. We shed love on you as often as we could. Since you weren't able to use your magic, you couldn't see us and so you didn't know we were there.

"Okayyyyy ..." Tilly was speechless.

Peony smiled. "We are here to show you the way to the Magic Realm and introduce you to the witches so you may learn how to use your powers."

Lance gestured to the archway. "If you are ready to go, we will escort you through this portal."

The archway began to get blurry, and a beautiful landscape of brilliant colors began to appear. Tilly couldn't resist. It was as if it were calling to her. It felt so much like home. So she followed them through.

THE MAGIC Realm was even more beautiful than she could have imagined. Trees, flowers, and beautiful creatures were everywhere. In the distance she could see a large glowing castle.

"That is where King Jerome lives," Peony told her. "You will meet him soon enough, but first we need to get to the Magic Shop. The witches are anxious to meet you." Peony laughed while flying circles around her.

A colorful cottage with banners flying from the roof stood past the next corner. On the front porch lay a beautiful gray wolf. As Tilly walked up the steps, the door flew open and a beautiful woman with long silver hair greeted her with open arms. Peony and Lance each gave her a quick kiss on her cheeks and waved goodbye.

"Welcome Tilly! Happy birthday! Today is the day we have all been waiting for. I am Thia. Come in and meet the rest of us."

And with that, Thia drew Tilly into the shop.

The shop was far larger on the inside than it was on the outside. It seemed to go on forever. All sorts of beautiful flowers, plants, bottles, and lovely things were stacked on shelves. Standing together and smiling were four more lovely ladies, all dressed in colorful clothing. There were no black hats or somber garments here. This was a place of beautiful magic.

Tilly then met the women who would help her find her power and become the witch she was always meant to be. They introduced themselves: Kimbalina, Kachina, Lorelei, Guinevere, and Thia. Their coven was the Witches of Glazedham.

The witches were more than happy to help her. Tilly was the daughter of their close friends Benedict and Rosalynne. They would give anything to help bring that family back together.

"All right! Let's get started, Luv," said Guinevere. "We already know that you have the ability to speak with animals but just to make sure it's not only adorable squirrels, let's invite Wolf in and see how you two get along."

She turned to the animal lying on the porch.

"Wolf, can you please come in and greet Tilly?"

The beautiful gray wolf sauntered in from the front porch. One could almost make out a smile showing on her face. "Good morning, Tilly," said Wolf. Tilly noticed right away that the greeting was not actually coming from Wolf's mouth, yet she could clearly hear it in her ear and in her head.

"Good morning, Wolf," Tilly said out loud.

Guinevere laid a hand on Tilly's shoulder and spoke. "Many animals cannot speak with their voices to make their words, but they can all make themselves heard with thought projection. They can both hear your voice and hear your mind speak, if needed. Some creatures such as crows and other birds can speak with their voices. There are so many others that can do this as well, and you will discover them as you go through your life as a witch."

"Try again with Wolf, but this time just use your mindspeak," said Thia.

"Wolf, you are looking quite lovely today. I am so glad to meet you." Tilly smiled as she used her mindspeak. Wolf did indeed smile this time and bowed with her front legs and head to the ground.

"Lady Tilly, you are gracious and lovely yourself. I look forward to a long friendship with you. Blessed be," said Wolf.

"Animals on Earthside will be just

the same," said Tilly. "You'll be able to communicate with all of them. But remember, some have issues and may not always be trusted. It just depends on what life has dealt them."

Thia continued: "You can also use mind speak with any Supernatural. But understand that it doesn't work with a human. They cannot hear you this way and you can't hear them*."

"We also already know that you can see and hear Supernaturals from the Earth side," said Kimbalina. "Your pixies that you just met this morning have been in your family for ages. They have kept your gardens and have watched over you since your father went away. We know that life has not been easy for you but know that they have kept you safe from harm and made sure you had what you needed. We have all had to be cautious and not expose you to those who would do you harm until the spell your mother used was lifted."

"But now, Tilly, you are more than capable of protecting yourself and you will be safe." Kachina hugged her. "King Jerome has asked that we tell you he is aware that you are here and will help in any way he can. He has ordered a search in the Dark Realm to find your parents and grandparents. It is time the truth be known and to arrange their release."

"And now, Tilly, let's see what other powers you have," Lorelei said. "Know that it is not a matter of us teaching you but just helping you to discover and understand what powers you have and what use they are to you."

It truly wasn't a matter of what powers she had. There seemed to be no limit. Tilly was handed a broom and was able to fly. She threw fire balls, water balls, and made rose petals fall from the sky. She stopped large objects flying at her in their tracks. She called the wind, the rain, thunder, and lighting. She disappeared and reappeared, she made objects disappear and reappear. She turned apples into oranges and back again. She knew without coaching what potions would be good for and how to brew them.

Many more Supernaturals dropped by throughout the day and Tilly met and greeted them all. She soon learned that elves are not so tiny, just a tad smaller than most humans. Witches come in all sizes and can be part of this or that.

Vampires are real but not thirsty for blood — in fact they are quite nice and beautiful to behold. Vampires have the ability to move at lightning speed, and they are not at all allergic to sunlight. They are always gifted musicians.

Werewolves are able to transform back and forth between animal and human shapes, and there are many other different types of shapeshifters.

Dragons and unicorns, talking trees, druids, Sasquatch and even ghosts came and went. There were even a few humans, but Tilly learned that humans could only enter through a portal and only if they were invited. One must be a Supernatural to enter the Magic Realm by simply willing oneself to be there.

At the end of the day, the witches had helped her discover what she had been gifted and who she was, the most powerful witch ever born. But most important of all,

they had thoroughly searched her heart
and found it as pure and kind as could be,
and the witches then knew that there would
never, ever be an evil bone in her body.

Present Day

Tilly is a witch who was born with great magic. She had not realized how powerful she was until just a few months before her twentieth birthday. Before then, she had lived in a big cardboard box with 125 squirrels she took care of, and in exchange her squirrels slept in the cardboard box with her so that she was warm, comfy, and wrapped in the softness of their fluffy tails. Tilly made sure they had all the nuts they could eat every day, and she protected them from predators and meanies.

One day, while riding her broom and searching for her squirrels' favorite acorns, she came upon a dog dressed like a hot dog. He was dancing and carrying a sign that was lit up with neon letters that said *Eat at*

Joe's Deli. The poor little guy looked so tired from all his dancing. A large man with a stick stood near him, and he would occasionally strike the poor dog with the stick if he slowed his dancing. Tilly flew by and then quickly turned her broom and landed next to the man.

"What are you doing? Who gives you the right to strike that sweet pup with a stick?" Tilly asked. The man turned to see a lovely young woman with red hair blowing, her emerald eyes looking dangerous as she glared at the man. She held her broom in such a way that he was afraid she was going to strike him with it.

"Oh, get lost!" he sneered. "This is my dog, and I can do anything I want with him. He answers only to me! Careful, or I will order him to attack you."

Now that Tilly was in full control of her powers, she had a few tricks up her sleeve. She slammed her broomstick on the ground at the man's feet and said, "Be still and do my will." And the mean man stood perfectly still.

One of Tilly's awesome powers was the

ability to speak with all animals, so she turned to the little dog and asked him: "Little pup. What is your name?"

The poor dog was trembling on his little legs. He was so exhausted.

"My name is Streetmeat," he replied. "This man promised me all the hot dogs I could eat if I wore his stupid sign and danced in front of his restaurant every day. But he only gives me one hot dog per day, and then he makes me sleep with a chain around my neck outside in the cold at night."

"That's no life for a dog! Do you want to continue dancing for this man? Would you like a better life?" Tilly asked.

"Any life would be better than this. Can you save me?" the dog asked with tears in his eyes.

Tilly gently scooped up Streetmeat, climbed up on her broom and flew away after leaving the man free to move again. He was shaking his fist angrily at her and the dog.

So, between her 125 squirrels and her new dog named Streetmeat, silly Tilly was never lonely, and her friends were never hungry.

How Tilly Was Able to Move Out of Her Box

One morning ... a good story *always* starts in the morning ... Tilly woke up in her cardboard box parked behind the very best deli in the state of California. Tilly's job was opening the deli, making and selling breakfast sandwiches. The pay wasn't much, but Streetmeat was getting fat on as many hot dogs as he could possibly eat. Tilly also had quite a few side jobs that required her skills of magic, which she was getting better and better at providing.

On that morning, Tilly had found a note, written on fine parchment paper, carefully taped to the outside of her cardboard box. The note read:

Dear Tilly,

*I need your help. I have a big
ghost problem. Please come to
the castle in the Magic Realm as
soon as possible.*

Respectfully, King Jerome

WELL, TILLY was never one to turn down
a plea for help, especially if it was followed
by *please*. Great manners always work
and most certainly when the good King
Jerome asked. So, after making sure
that her squirrels had their morning nuts
and Streetmeat was full of hot dogs, she
grabbed her broom and was on her way.

She arrived in the Magic Realm easily.
Magic is everywhere if you know where to
look, and a good broom ride will get you
there quickly. She landed at the castle door
and knocked. The door opened with lots of
creaking and groaning and moaning. Tilly
was not surprised to find on the other side
of the door two tiny fairies who seemed to
be a wee bit exhausted from pulling open
such a huge, heavy door.

"Good morning. My name is Tilly, and I'm

here to meet with his Royal Highness," Tilly said. The fairies floated around her face so fiercely that Tilly 's hair was blowing into her eyes.

"Oh, thank you so much for coming. Please come in," they said. "Our master will be so grateful to see you." They pulled her in gently by her hair to lead her further into the great hallway.

Tilly looked to the left and saw another hallway that was long and filled with the usual paintings of royalty. She looked to the right, and she saw yet another hallway, this one dark and forbidding. At the very end, she could almost see what appeared to be gray shadows, floating and making the loudest and most unpleasant noise she had ever heard. She put her fingers in her ears to make the noise quieter, but it made no difference.

The owner of the castle, His Majesty Jerome the Great, chose this moment to appear before her. King Jerome was a young king, about twenty in Earthside years. He was tall, with blond hair, and very handsome. His ears were pointed, which gave away the fact that he was also Elfin. Elfin magic was not to be messed with, but in this case, his powers were not going to help the situation.

Jerome shouted at Tilly. "I have been hoping to meet you, Tilly. Thank you so much for coming. I am so happy to make your acquaintance."

"Sorry, I didn't get that," Tilly replied, yelling over the sound of the awful music. Jerome threw up his hands and then grabbed her by the wrist and pulled her into a room far down the left hallway where the music wasn't as loud. It was now at least possible to hear each other.

"Wow, that is some loud awful music, Your Highness. How can you bear it?" Tilly asked.

"I can't take it anymore," he answered. "I will restore your fortune and your family mansion on the Earthside if you get rid of these loud ghosts."

He went on to explain that he had invited them personally to play their music at his crowning ceremony many years ago and they had died in a terrible fire on that very night.

"The Knight Walkers, being Supernatural vampires, have been playing music since the fifth century. They always adapted their music to the changing times. That night there was a fire due to some electrical failure with the sound equipment and they all perished. Now I can't even throw them out because they are ghosts."

Tilly knew exactly what to do, but it was going to take some strong magic to rescue them and silence the horrible noise they were making.

"I can have them out by tomorrow, Your Highness," Tilly said, smiling at the king. But first I will need a few things and a little help from my friends. I will return shortly."

Then off she flew to her friends' magic shop.

The Witches of Glazedham's Magic Shop

Now there are magic shops, and then there are big magic shops. The witches of Glazedham had spent years together as a coven and had collected countless artifacts of splendor and powerful magic items. The shop was full of potions and candles, spell books, brooms, and recipe books; it would be rare indeed, if they didn't have what was needed to cast a spell.

Tilly landed at the door with a soft graceful swoop. The door opened magically, and there stood all five of the witches. Tilly was delighted to find them all together. They in turn were so happy to see her. Each one gave her a warm, welcoming hug.

Each witch was gifted with her own specialty of magic. Guinevere was tall and graceful, and with long gray hair and a slight British accent. Her gift was manifesting. She could make things appear and disappear whenever needed. She was a cosmic witch. She worked with the energy of the planets, stars, and galaxy. Rumor was that she was once the Queen Guinevere, but no one could ever say.

Thia, also tall with flowing silver hair, was well known as the mother and protector of all animals. She was a crystal witch and worked with the energy of crystals and stones. She also understood the speech of animals and the animals understood her. It was rare if there wasn't some creature nearby, or in her lap. Always her gray wolf was by her side.

Kimbalina was a guardian of the Earth and a fairy witch. Trees gave way for her, flowers grew at her feet if she stayed too long in one place, her potions from teas and herbs were legendary in the magical realm. Kimbalina, being part fairy, was a bit smaller than her sisters. When she got very excited or angry, her tiny golden wings would pop out and begin to flutter.

Next there was Lorelei. Lorelei loved to make beautiful art that seemed to come alive with color, but her strongest and most handy gift was healing. She was an elemental witch using the natural elements of earth, wind, fire, and water to cast her magic.

And finally, Kachina. Kachina had the ability to speak with spirits. She could read tarot and revealed just the right answers for those who ask. Her magic was aligned with her Native American heritage. In fact, her name meant spirit in the language of the Cherokee. Kachina was a moon witch and used the energy of the moon in all its phases to cast her spells.

All of the witches had the same beautiful tattoo on their right forearms. It was a crescent moon with a lovely broom. This was a symbol of their sisterhood in magic. The broom tattoo itself was their own personal magical way of carrying their actual broom. It was very handy, and whenever needed they could make their brooms appear just by tapping the broom on their arms three times. Their brooms would then appear in their right hands. Not a single one of them ever wore a pointed witch hat.

"Tilly! What brings you to our shop on such a lovely day," Kachina exclaimed. "And how are all of your 125 squirrels and Streetmeat the hot-dog dog?"

"The squirrels are safe and sound and holding down our cardboard box," Tilly told the little witch. "Streetmeat is just fine and putting on weight from all the hot dogs he is getting,"

Then she got down to the reason for her visit. "I am in need of some rather unusual items. I am hoping you either have them stowed away somewhere or might be able to manifest them."

Kachina nodded,

"I have a job to help King Jerome to rid himself of some very loud ghosts," Tilly went on. "Remember the Knight Walkers? They all perished in a fire quite a few years ago and seem to be trapped in spirit limbo. Their spirits are so loud no one in the castle can hear themselves think. Poor King Jerome is desperate."

"Oh," sighed Kachina. "The Knight Walkers have been around for centuries, since King Arthur's time in the fifth or sixth century. They were always so good, and my goodness they were such handsome vampires. It's too bad they died in the Magic Realm, which is also known as the Dark Realm. That's why they are trapped, because it's in between."

She paused and Tilly waited.

"I think you may need my help communicating with them," Kachina continued. "They are probably so confused and locked into a loop playing the same song over and over. They have no idea that it sounds loud and awful because all of their equipment was damaged in the fire."

Tilly agreed with her on the offer of help. "I would like all of your help if you are available," she said. "King Jerome has promised to restore my family home and fortune if I can help him."

She handed a sheet of paper to Kachina. "Here is my list of supplies. I need a set of drums, three guitars, one base and two lead electrics, all in working order. I will also need a magic sound system."

All of the witches were excited to help

gather the supplies for Tilly and included what they would need for their own magic. Finally, when everything was ready, they magically compressed the band equipment into very small packages, and each witch carried a piece in their pocket.

"All right, I think we have everything we need, and we are ready to fly," Kimbalina announced.

Tilly stood outside on the porch, waiting for them with her broom in hand. The other witches stepped out of the shop, and Thia commanded her wolf to stay and guard the shop as she locked the door. Tilly wondered where their brooms might be and was amazed to see each witch tap gently on her right forearm and their broom tattoos magically disappear from their arms and their actual brooms appear in their right hands.

Off they all flew to the castle in the Magic Realm.

Restoring Peace and Quiet to King Jerome

King Jerome was waiting patiently at the drawbridge of the castle. It was obvious he was happy to see Tilly and her friends. The witches landed and stood waiting with their brooms in their right hands.

"Welcome ladies. Thank you for helping. I know I am in the best of hands," King Jerome said. "Follow me this way."

He ushered them toward the castle door and led them down the long hallway. At the end of the hallway, they entered the ballroom. At the very end of the ballroom, they saw a stage set up with really damaged band equipment. The drums were charred and burned and there were holes filled with spiderwebs. The guitars were somewhat melted, with strings that were no longer tight, and some were even missing. The speakers were melted with electrical cords connecting to nothing. Yet still the equipment was making a terrible noise.

They could just make out the gray shapes of ghosts, floating in and out of existence, appearing to be passionately playing away. The witches could almost make out a song, but it was hard to hear over the racket of the instruments. Also, it was painfully earsplitting.

King Jerome stood there with hands on his hips. "This is what I hear all day, every day. It never stops. We are all losing our minds. They don't seem to hear me. I've tried throwing away the equipment, but it all magically appears the minute we have the stage cleared. The ghosts, they never really leave."

Kachina listened to the noise. She explained that they were stuck in a loop in another dimension. The instruments were not Supernatural but were magicked. Therefore, they would not allow themselves to be moved, unless it was by the band members.

Removing this noise was going to take the gifts of magic that all the witches possessed. They had to start with the ghosts. They needed to be pulled back into the Magic Realm. Then they needed to be restored and healed. Next, the magic had to be removed from the damaged equipment and fresh magic added to their new equipment.

Finally, the Knight Walkers could move on with their fame and fortune to wherever they wished. Then King Jerome could finally have some peace and quiet. Tilly could move out of her box and into a mansion and have a fortune to feed all of her animals. And the Witches of Glazedham could also move on to new adventures.

"All right ladies, let's begin. Brooms out!" Each witch, except for Tilly, lightly tapped her right forearm, and their brooms disappeared from their arms and appeared in their right hands. Tilly simply stood ready with her broom. A little smile appeared on her face. She really admired the simple magic way they carried their brooms and always kept them available.

Guinevere began to manifest a large ball

of magic in her hands and directed it to each witch's broom. This would boost the power needed to pull the band members safely back to the Magic Realm.

Tilly took over and commanded the witches, "brooms up!" Each turned her broom so the stick rested on the ground. "Summon your Magic!" Each witch slammed her broomstick firmly on the ground. A roll of magic began forming, glowing in red and green, yellow, and blue. "Cast the spell," called Kimbalina.

The witches began to chant. "Spirits, trapped on the other side, we compel and command you to join us in this Magic Realm."

The ghosts began to twist and spin crazily around the room. They dived in and out between the witches. Finally, they landed on the stage, looking a bit more solid, but still gray and a ghostlike.

Kachina stepped forward and aimed her broomstick in a magic stream. She commanded the band members to stop and listen: "We mean you no harm and want no harm in return. Can you understand me?"

The ghost known as Christian nodded his head and smiled a ghoulish green grin. "I understand and best of all I can hear you. We have been in a place where no matter how hard we tried, all we could do was play our music over and over and over again, it seemed no one could hear us. We welcome your help."

The other ghosts nodded in agreement. Tilly said: "Stay as solid as you can. The magic should be helping with that. Lorelei will heal each of you. Then you should be able to hear us all. Best of all you will have your solid Supernatural bodies back. But first, we need to silence those instruments."

Tilly aimed her broom at the burned-up mess and yelled, "stop the music!" And just like that there was sweet, sweet silence.

Lorelei appeared before Christian and gently placed her broomstick to his forehead. Healing magic streamed from her broom and into his body. Almost instantly, his body became more solid, and he cleared his throat. His voice was rough, and tears began to form in his eyes.

"Beautiful witches, how can we thank

you for rescuing us? We are all eternally grateful."

Lorelei was already on to healing the rest of the band members, so Tilly answered. "Live your lives well and do no harm to others. And always lend a hand up when you come across someone in need. That is our creed as Supernaturals."

Christian turned to his other band members and hugged each one of them. They all looked as they did before they perished in the fire so many centuries ago: handsome, healthy, and well-dressed rock stars.

Then they noticed their burnt and damaged band instruments.

Tilly saw their sad faces and started collecting the new pieces of instruments from the witches' pockets. Tilly placed each new replacement on the damaged piece, and each new piece grew and merged with the damaged items, leaving the stage filled with a new gleaming sound system.

Finally, there stood before the witches four musicians with a new magical shining sound system, drums, and guitars.

Well, of course, the Knight Walkers just had to try everything out and play for the king again. Soon the witches, the king, all of the king's family, members of his court, and even his staff were rocking out to the fabulous sounds of the Knight Walkers.

As Tilly was preparing to leave, Christian and his band members caught up with her.

"Tilly," said Christian," is there anything we can do to thank you for rescuing us? We have plenty of time on our hands right now. Having been gone so long, it's going to take some time to book more dates to play."

Tilly thought for a moment. "Yes. I was just handed back the deed to my family's mansion that is in need of some repairs. I could use some help with that."

The band agreed that they would need a place to stay temporarily and would be honored to help out with the repairs. They turned to the king and bowed. Christian said, "Your highness, thank you for helping to rescue us. We are once again all eternally in your debt."

Tilly noticed something odd when he spoke. While it seemed he was addressing the king, his eyes were actually on Guinevere. Guinevere quietly turned her body toward the band and put her finger to her lips. So off the witches went, to their different corners of the Earth, to their regular Earthside mortal lives, to the families they loved, and who saw them far differently than they were in the Magic Realm. Mortals wouldn't ever understand someone flying on a broom, creating magic that streamed out of their hands, sprouting wings, or even pointy ears or teeth. Humans would be very surprised to know there were those who were really something more than what they saw every day.

It was a wonderful thing that the Magic Realm was just a thought away, and as a Supernatural one could come and go from there as easily as breathing.

Tilly Can't Find Her Broom

Tilly woke up with a start. Something was quite out of sorts. She just couldn't think exactly what it could be. Sitting up and stretching in her bed and sliding her feet to the floor, she shuffled to the bathroom, absentmindedly scratching her right arm.

She brushed her teeth and rinsed her mouth. Then she attacked her thick mane of red curls and settled for a black bow to keep her hair back in a ponytail. She dressed in jeans and a long-sleeve T-shirt and headed downstairs.

It was another day of remodeling at the mansion, where she lived with 125 friends, who were squirrels, who each had their own tiny, personal bedroom. Her dog, Streetmeat, also had his very own room complete with his magical refrigerator, which was continuously filled with his very favorite pre-made beef hot dogs. She also had helpful roommates, the band called the Knight Walkers, who were there to help make much needed repairs.

She could hear sawing and hammering somewhere below. That could only be the band members making themselves useful. Tilly walked into the kitchen and poured herself a big cup of coffee. Everyone knew they needed to be quiet and give her peace until she had her first cup down.

She stepped out to the garden with a cup in hand and watched the family of pixies tending to the flowers. It made her smile as the little creatures flickered from plant to plant. Pixies have always tended gardens and all the plants and trees on the Earthside, but one must be Supernatural to actually see them. Most people would just assume that their own efforts of watering, pruning and the sunshine were responsible for the beauty of nature. If they only knew the truth.

She greeted the little family with a wave

and a happy good morning. "Good morning, Tilly," Peony said. Peony was the mother of a brood of 12 little pixie children. Their father was Lance, and he was currently helping the youngest child with a small bucket of pollen that was being prepared for the roses. Peony flew close to Tilly and landed on her shoulder.

"Tilly, so glad you are up. We are so happy for you to have returned to this old house. It's been a while, and it needs some attention. I have prepared a list of supplies we need for the vegetable garden. Do you think we could have it fulfilled by the end of the day?"

The list magically appeared in front of Tilly and floated into her hand.

Tilly looked over the list. "No problem, Peony. This won't take long. I have some other requests from Christian. I think I will just pop over to the Magic Realm to gather everything."

Again, Tilly rubbed at her right arm. It felt, well, maybe a little itchy. Perhaps, she thought, she should give Lorelei a call and see if Kimbalina or Lorelei might have a cure for the itch. Meanwhile, it was time for a quick breakfast, and then she would fetch her broom and be off.

Tilly finished her breakfast, and then found Christian busily pulling up floorboards on the front porch. "I need your supply list and then I am off to the Magic Realm to gather everything."

Christian pulled the list from his pocket. "Hey there! Good morning! It's a big list. How will you transport everything to get it all here?" he asked.

"Easy peasy," she replied. "I will just make everything small and fit it all into a magic sack. You know, like Santa does."

She turned the corner by the front door where she had left her broom the night before. But the broom wasn't there.

"Well, this is odd," she said to herself.

SHE BEGAN to search the house, asking everyone if they had moved it, or used it for actual sweeping, maybe? But no one had any answers. Meanwhile, her arm began to really, really itch. Now, she was really getting upset. No broom, lots to do and her arm was bugging her.

She decided to give Lorelei a call in the human way and grabbed her cell phone. Thankfully, Lorelei picked up the call immediately.

"Hey, good morning, Lorelei," Tilly said, still absentmindedly rubbing her arm.

Lorelei replied: "Tilly, it's always good to hear from you. How are you? How are the repairs on the mansion coming along?"

Tilly scowled. "Well, I would like to say 'perfectly,' but this morning things are not quite going as planned. I can't seem to find my broom, and now I have this weird itch on my right arm. I was wondering if you or Kimbalina might have a potion for it. Then I guess I will need to have a new broom delivered from the Magic Shop. I will need that before I can even begin my chores for the day."

Lorelei chuckled. "Tilly, I think I can help with all your problems! Have you looked at your arm this morning?"

"Well ... no ... hang on a sec ... what? How did this get here?" Tilly wondered out loud. On her right arm was a beautiful tattooed crescent moon with a broom that looked just like her own missing broom.

Lorelei chuckled again. "Happy Late Birthday from the Witches of Glazedham. We wanted to give you something special. Kachina bestowed it on you when she hugged you goodbye yesterday. We hope you love it. If the tattoo is bothering you, just pop in and we will give you something to soothe it. To use the tattoo, just tap on the broom three times with intention and your broom will be manifest in your hand. To return it, tap three times again on your arm and it will return. It's that simple."

Tilly was surprised and delighted by this wonderful gift.

"I love it. I am eternally grateful. Thank you to all of you."

Lorelei added: "We also wish to invite you to be a member of the Witches of Glazedham. Will you accept?"

Tilly was over the moon with joy. She loved these witches like sisters. "What a way to turn my day around. I can't wait to see all of you," Tilly said. "I will be there shortly."

Tilly hung up the phone, rolled up her sleeve and gently tapped three times. Her broom instantly appeared in her hand. Squealing with delight, off she flew.

Tilly Goes Swat Team on the Dark Realm

The mansion was quickly looking like a home full of love and happiness again.

Each day Tilly would wake with a smile and listen for a moment to the sounds around her. She heard the squirrels chatter as they happily went from tree to tree outside and then back inside the house. They had been provided many access points to come and go as they pleased. They were part of her family after all.

Streetmeat's little feet were clicking on the oak floor as he waited patiently for her to wake up.

Below she heard the vampires as they hammered and sawed and laughed among themselves. They were the busiest men she had ever met. Who knew that although they had spent centuries playing beautiful music they could also be such excellent carpenters. Blessed be, she thought. I am a lucky witch!

The pixie family was also already up and at work with the garden. Tilly knew that when she entered the kitchen, there would be a fresh basket of produce ready to prepare for the day's meals.

Tilly sat up and smiled at Streetmeat. "Good morning, little dude." She bent down to scoop him up to her bed and sat him beside her. "What are your plans for the day?"

Streetmeat cuddled closer and answered. "I have no big plans for myself, but I would love to help you with yours, my friend. Lance the pixie has already been knocking on the door and asks to speak with you right away."

"Now that is unusual! I hope everything is all right."

While the pixies were most welcome, they rarely entered the house. They much preferred the fresh outdoors no matter what the weather was like. She frowned a little in concern.

For some reason she hesitated as to

what to wear for the day. Bright colors just didn't seem right. She grabbed some black leather jeans, black t-shirt, and sturdy boots. After a good fresh face wash, teeth brushed, and hair pulled back in a pony, she went downstairs. She found as she entered the kitchen that she was not the only one who was feeling the need to dress in black. There sat Christian, her favorite vampire and dearest friend, dressed almost identically to her.

"Well, I am glad I got the mental memo, too," he smiled. "I wonder what this is all about." He poured her a cup of coffee and handed it to her. "My intuition says we are dressed this way for a reason."

Tilly sipped her coffee and agreed with a nod. "Anybody else in the house going dark?" she mused.

"Nope, it's just you and me so far," he replied. But then the pixie Lance appeared at the back door and, behold, he was also dressed for combat. Tilly opened the door, and he fluttered in. "What the heck is going on, Lance? Why are we dressed like this?"

"I am sorry Miss Tilly; I have good news

and maybe bad news. I received word from his Highness King Jerome that your family has been located in the Dark Realm. The King has ordered the three of us to go in to rescue them." Lance stood on the tabletop, looking like the most fierce and dangerous pixie one could imagine.

"Well, that is good news my little friend! What is the bad news?" Tilly wondered.

"The bad news is that it won't be easy." Lance looked downcast. "I must be honest: I have never been to the Dark Realm before. It's, it's ... well it is very dark. There is no joy, there are no smiley souls, it's full of evil and big ... ugly ... meanies."

Christian and Tilly stole looks at each other and sat up straighter. Christian knew exactly what it would be like. He had been rescued from there less than a year ago. He and his vampire band had spent a long time there as ghosts. If anyone was up to this task, it was him. He would do anything for his friend Tilly. He didn't like the idea of going back either, but it was what needed to be done.

Tilly had no fear of going. All she could

think of was the joy of seeing her father, meeting her mother and grandparents, and bringing them home. She couldn't wait to get started. Her greatest weapon would be her love for them. The fact that she was a very powerful witch wouldn't hurt either.

"What do we have to do, Lance? How do we get there?" Tilly was already on her feet as she grabbed a backpack to fill with supplies.

Christian was also grabbing a bag and on his way to his room to search for his weapons. It had been a very long time since he had needed such things, but he knew how to use a sword and dagger, and as a vampire he had even more talents. Lance spoke: "The King wants to meet with us first. I believe he is going as well. He says it is about time he meets with the King of the Dark Realm. If everything goes as he hopes, we may not have to battle our way in or out."

The three of them said goodbye to their loved ones, and then standing close together and in the blink of an eye, they found themselves in the royal presence of King Jerome.

King Jerome, also dressed in black, looked magnificent, fierce, and ready to do battle if needed. He was armed with a gleaming golden sword.

The King greeted them with a smile. "Tilly, it is good to see you again. I trust that Lance has briefed you. I have received information from his highness King Drake of the Dark Realm. He has located your family. They are being held by Lord Rendon, one of the High Lords of the Dark Realm.

"Lord Rendon thinks he can trade them for you, Tilly. Your birth and great power were predicted long ago. He has been planning to use you for your extraordinary gifts all this time. It was he that caused a spell to misfire and cause the death of hundreds in our Magic Realm. He plotted to have your grandparents and your father blamed for it all, and then he arranged to have them banished to his Realm so he would have better control over the outcome of your future. I am sad to say that your mother's parents were also involved in this. My own father was killed because of his plans.

"It was a true blessing that your mother escaped to Earthside. Your being born there was the best thing that could have happened. Your parents were able to conceal you from him long enough for you to receive all of your talents at once. Now you will always be able to defend yourself against evil.

"He has no idea who he is up against. The witches tell me that your magic is so pure and powerful that you can't be harmed." The King paced as he spoke.

"We still need a plan and I think I know where to start."

The King unrolled a map of the Dark Realm out on his table.

"Christian, your time as a spirit in the Dark Realm should help us find our way to his hiding place. Don't you agree?" he asked. Christian nodded.

"Yes, your highness, I was everywhere looking for a way back. I know every little dark hole that wretched place has to offer. Lord Rendon is familiar to me, and I already know where he hides and exactly how to get there."

The King smiled. "I knew you would, Christian, your good heart will lead us all to the rescue."

King Jerome turned to Lance. "Your size will be of great assistance to us, my small but mighty little friend. I am glad to see that you brought your sword. I have here a potion that you will need. A small drop on your sword and tiny prick to the neck of each guard and they will be fast asleep. They will never see you coming. I have seen how fast you are."

Lance puffed his chest out proudly. "I will give my life for the Carruthers family, Sir. They have always treated me like their own. It is my honor."

The King then turned to Tilly. "Tilamia Carruthers, I know you just came into your amazing gifts of witchcraft, but know that no one can match you. The goodness and kindness in your heart will defeat this enemy in ways you can't even imagine."

Tilly wanted to hug her King, but she knew that was so inappropriate. Instead, she simply smiled her smile and gave him a hard punch in the arm, probably even more inappropriate but it seemed the right thing to do at the moment. King Jerome winced at the punch and rubbed his arm, then laughed at her.

"Owww. ... I have no doubts we will succeed, so let's be off," King Jerome commanded.

The Dark Realm was so different from the Magic Realm. The air was heavy and smelled like rancid fish oil. There were no clouds in the sky. Instead, a thin layer of fog floated at different levels over the terrain. No flowers, no colorful flags, no smiles on the faces of the people. The village they had transported to was dreary and depressing. It was indeed a most awful place. Everyone they passed was dressed in black. Not even brown or gray was present. No one smiled, no one made eye contact. Even the children seemed just as pitiful and sad as the adults.

"Well," thought Tilly, "all this explains the special ops look we decided to wear today. We blend right in."

"Let's get this party started," she said to her brave team.

They followed Christian through alleys

and dark streets. Everything looked the same. It was amazing that Christian seemed to know his way. But of course, he had floated around for years while he was a ghost exploring and looking for a way out.

Finally, they came to a small fortress. It was by no means a castle but still it looked dark and forbidding. It was surrounded by a wall with at least 30 guards. Each guard was armed with an assortment of spears and swords. The only way in seemed to be through a heavy gate.

King Jerome took the lead and marched forward. He banged on the gate with his sword. "Good day," he shouted. "We are here to see Lord Rendon."

"Who goes there?" a guard bellowed.

"I, King Jerome, from the Magic Realm. I come with my guard and my witch. I am ordering you to surrender the Carruthers family members to us immediately," he commanded.

Lance had disappeared and had already found his own way into the fortress. No one seemed to notice that the guards were beginning to doze off at their posts. More armed guards appeared out of nowhere with weapons trained on the King, his guard, and his witch.

Lord Rendon also appeared from nowhere and approached them out of the dark. He was surrounded by even more guards.

"Surrender the Carruthers family to you? They murdered innocent people. Wasn't your own father killed during their disaster? It's impossible. Be off before I lock you up as well, Your Highness," the Lord sneered.

"You will do no such thing. Do you think I don't know about your treachery? Do you think I have no proof of the spells you cast that caused the death of my people and my father, the King? You are holding innocent citizens of my realm and I demand you release them. Resist me and I will bring you back for trial as well." Tilly was in awe of the power her friend the King commanded.

Lord Rendon laughed and gestured around him. "There are three of you—a helpless King, one guard and a skinny witch. I have over a hundred trained warriors, all with weapons trained on you. You are my prisoners now," he laughed.

As the Lord glanced around to all his men, he was surprised to see that only ten of his guards remained standing; all the rest were cuddled up like little sleeping babies snoring away at their posts. And while he was surprised that most of his guards had passed out on the ground, he ordered his remaining guards to seize them.

It was time for Tilly to act. She quickly cast a dome of protection around the three of them. None of the guards' weapons could penetrate the magic. Lord Rendon suddenly realized who that skinny witch was.

"Well, well. What do I have here? Welcome, Tilamia Carruthers. You look just look like your lovely mother except for the color of your hair. Thank you for walking right into my fortress. You have made my life much easier; I don't have to come to find you. Now, you'll be my witch."

The Lord cast out with his own evil magic and tried to break through the protection that Tilly had cast. But of course, it was holding up just fine. Tilly decided to reach out toward this evil smelly man and showed him what else she could do with her magic.

By now all the guards were down and unconscious. Lance had done a most excellent job of putting them to sleep. Tilly held her arms forward, made a magical gesture with her hands and the Lord was suddenly raised off the ground and held steady about thirty feet in the air. No matter how hard he struggled, he couldn't escape.

"Hold him there, Tilly, and we will fetch your family," the King said.

Lance, Christian and King Jerome dashed into the fortress and disappeared. Christian knew exactly where to go to find the family in the dungeons beneath the fortress.

While they were gone, Tilly held Lord Rendon in the air. All the while he pleaded with her, promising her riches and splendor if she released him. He offered to free her family and let her help him rule all the Dark Realm. He knew ways to destroy the King of the Dark Realm. They could even be married. *Blah, blah, blah.* The more he talked, the more certain she was that he was going to have a nice, fast, hard fall on the way down.

Finally, after all the years of waiting, there stood her father, her mother, and her grandparents. Who to hug first? It was settled quickly with the entire family holding her in the center of one big giant hugfest.

The King signaled Tilly to drop the now-sobbing Lord Rendon. He did indeed land hard from such a height.

"Oops, I think I heard something break," Tilly laughed. Yes, she was all about goodness and everything, but this man had caused so much pain and sadness that if he broke his butt, she could fix it for him later.

The King then instructed the family to transport to one more place in the Dark Realm and then they could all go home. They headed for the King of the Dark Realm's Castle.

King Drake was expecting them. All of them ... especially Lord Rendon.

"So, Lord Rendon, I understand that you have ways to destroy me? You would rule in my place. I think it's time that you get a tour of my dungeons."

King Drake loomed over the cowering Lord. He turned to King Jerome. "Your

Highness, thank you for bringing this matter to my attention. I am glad to have helped you discover the location of this unfortunate family and get to the bottom of the crime committed by Lord Rendon. He will be punished." He bowed to King Jerome.

King Jerome shook his hand "Thank you King Drake. Let's plan on meeting soon under better circumstances and discover ways to help each other with ways to provide our realms with the very best we can offer."

King Drake nodded in agreement. "Yes, I believe it's time for my realm to welcome some light into our hearts and homes."

The Carruthers Family Heads Home

The first stop for the rescued family was
to gather at the castle of the Magic Realm.
King Jerome officially pardoned each family
member and sent out announcements
throughout the Realm to everyone to let
them know a dark deed had been revealed
and the Carruthers family were found
innocent and had returned safe and sound.

While the grandparents Lila and Thadeus
Carruthers planned to live in the Magic
Realm as before, they couldn't yet part with
their beloved family and agreed to go to
Earthside to stay for a while.

The family magicked themselves back to
Earthside and to the mansion where Tilly
and her father had once lived together.

Tilly had so much to say to her parents,

she wasn't sure where to start. Her parents also were unable to take their eyes off their child. It had been twelve long years since Benedict had seen Tilly. He had never expected to be away so long. He had no way of knowing what had happened in his absence. He had been fooled by the family that he had chosen to care for her. He was filled with so much regret over what she had to suffer while he was away. Lance had filled him in on how the family had taken advantage of the funds and the lack of care for Tilly and their lovely home. No revenge was needed as magic had a way of working things out when the flow of goodness was diverted.

Rosalynne had not seen her child for all of twenty years. She had not been there to watch her grow into the beautiful young woman who stood before her. When her parents had abducted Rosalynne and taken her to the Dark Realm with them, Tilly had been just a day old. There was no time to even kiss her goodbye. All she could do was cast a spell to hide her magic and then secure her baby in a drawer so that her parents had no idea where she was. And no matter what they did to her, she never confessed to them where she had hidden her child.

Now, this beautiful young lady stood before her. Her mother could see her own face on her. Tilly's hair was not blond like her mother's but the beautiful rich red mahogany like her father's side of the family. She was tall and healthy and moved with grace. At this moment, she was regarding her mother with the same curious gazes. Tilly and her parents were about to have their private reunion.

Silently, the three of them joined hands and moved to the vacant gathering room. It wasn't the time for tears any longer. They were together as a family.

They talked of how it was for Tilly as she grew up, which was the first thing on her father's and mother's minds. They were filled with grief and remorse that they had not been able to watch over their daughter and give her the love she deserved.

What they discovered as Tilly talked about her life is that she never, ever once felt that she was not loved or cared for. She could feel their love over all the distance that had been placed between them. She always knew that they would be together and simply lived with patience and doing her best to keep that hope in her heart. Her parents soon realized that the magic that Tilly had been born with had also equipped her with a good kind heart. It would always keep her on a path of greatness and what was good for all.

There was a light tap on the door and Benedict opened it to find that the whole household had gathered. Peony, Lance and their 12 children fluttered in and flew around the three of them. His parents entered carrying trays of sweets. Exactly one hundred and twenty-five squirrels scampered in and out between their legs. Christian and his band of Vampires entered carrying more trays of meats, cheese, breads, and fruit. Even Streetmeat strolled in pulling a cart full of his favorite hot dogs, ready to share with his family.

The future looked dazzling for this unusual family and Tilly couldn't wait to see what would happen next. She already knew that her magic was not for her to sit around to watch the world go by.

Meanwhile, she was going to have some cake!

The End
— or Is It?

ABOUT THIS BOOK: You've never met a witch like Tilly! Tilamia Carruthers had an ideal childhood growing up with her father, Benedict. When Tilly was 8, her father told her two secrets that changed her life: First, Tilly's parents were powerful witches and Tilly would inherit those powers when she was 20. Second and best of all, Benedict had finally found Tilly's mother, Rosalynne, in the Dark Realm and was leaving on a dangerous mission to rescue her. While she waits for her father to return, Tilly survives a sinister human foster family and learns to command her many magical powers, including talking to animals and meeting beings from other realms. Will she ever see her father again and finally meet her mother?

ABOUT THE AUTHOR: Kat Walker is a retired photographer. Using her imagination has always been a big part of her life. Tilly came to be through the imaginations of Kat and her twin grandsons. During their bedtime story times, the boys always prefer the tales they and their Nana invent together. This is the first time Kat and her grandsons have put Tilly's adventures into a book for everyone to enjoy.

Made in the USA
Las Vegas, NV
21 July 2024

92718897R00056